Zia the Orc

Janet Burchett & Sara Vogler

Illustrated by Lynne Willey

Tamarind Ltd

Sponsored by **NASUWT**

“I’m going to be an orchestra when I grow up,” said Zia.

“You mean an organist,” giggled her brother, Glen.

“Or a trumpeter?” suggested Mum.

“Why not be a drummer?” said Dad.

“The electric guitar,” said Gran, “That’s what I like.”

“No, ” said Zia, “I’m going to be an orchestra.”

Zia had a plan.

She hunted round in the shed.

She found a great big box
and took it up to her bedroom.

Then she went to look for Mum.
She was mending the washing machine.

"Can I borrow these?" asked Zia.

"Just don't make a mess," mumbled Mum.

She found Dad.
He was on the shed roof.

"Can I borrow this stick?" Zia called.
"Just for today."

"Help yourself," replied Dad,
"I'm busy."

Zia asked Gran for some hairpins.
"OK," said Gran.
"What are you up to?" asked Glen.
"Never you mind," replied Zia.
"Don't fight, kids," begged Gran.

She borrowed the dog's favourite squeaky toy.

Zia collected some rubber bands, a ruler and a shoe box.

Her family wondered why she kept offering round the biscuits.

“Gran, won’t you have another one?” she asked.

“I’m full darling. There’s only so many biscuits your old Gran can eat.”

“I’ll have the last two,” called Glen.

Zia found the blower left over from her party.
"This sounds good!"

When it came to lunch time, one or two things had gone missing...

and Zia ate four yoghurts,
which was odd, because
she didn't like yoghurt.

After lunch, Zia disappeared.

"Where's she gone?" asked Gran.

"What's happened to Zia?" asked Dad.

"Perhaps she's ill from eating too much yoghurt!" laughed Glen.

"Strange," said Mum.

They went and listened outside her bedroom door.

PING!
BANG!
CRASH!

Late in the afternoon, Zia came out of her room.

"There will be a concert in five minutes!
Get your tickets here," she announced grandly.

Everyone bought their tickets.
Then came a lot of crashing and clattering
as Zia came down the stairs.

“A concert,” called a voice from the hall.
“Performed by Zia the Orchestra.”

The next day Dad went to look for Zia.
“Would you like this drum for your orchestra?”
Zia was so busy she couldn’t answer.

Mum found Zia in her bedroom.

“I thought you might like my old recorder. I played it at school.”

“Thanks Mum,” Zia said without looking up.

Glen took Zia his old keyboard.

"You can have this, Sis. I don't use it any more," he said with a friendly smile.

"Can you help me with this?" she asked.

Gran went to look for Zia.

"Would you like a guitar lesson?" she asked.

"Maybe later," Zia said politely.

Zia was busy.

“I’ve changed my mind,” she said.
“I’m going to be a fire brigade!”

Zia's instruments

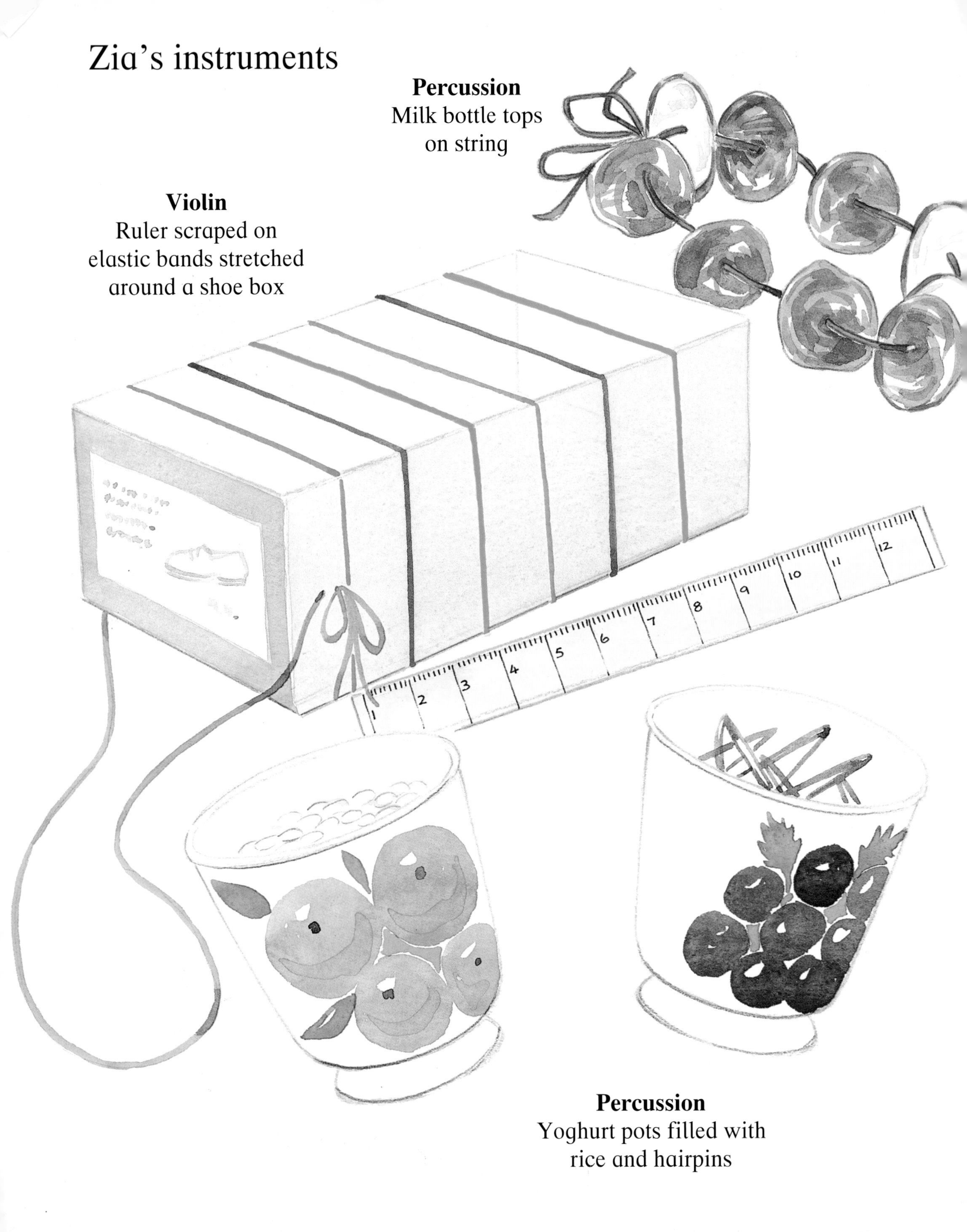

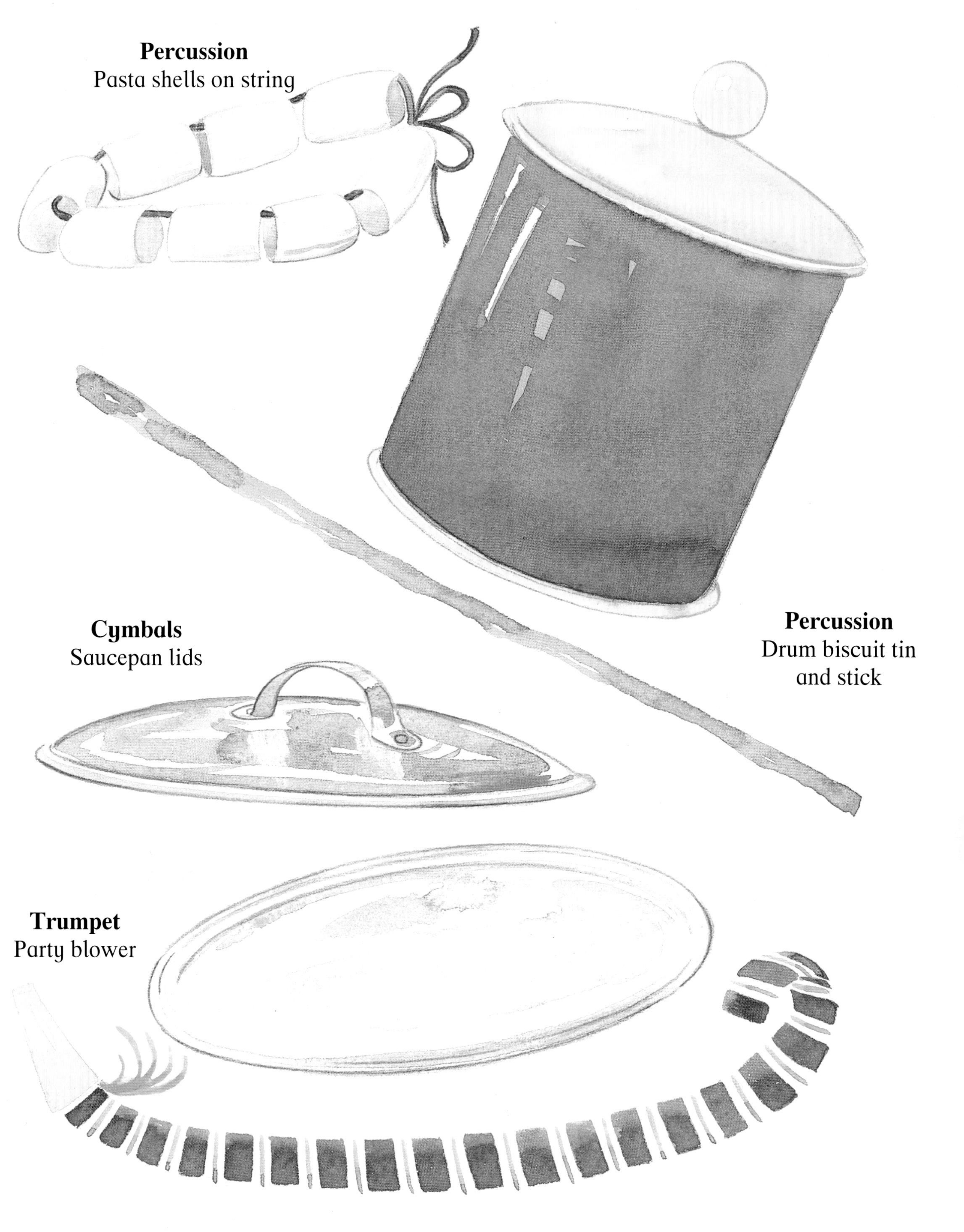
Percussion
Pasta shells on string
Percussion
Drum biscuit tin
and stick
Cymbals
Saucepan lids
Trumpet
Party blower

OTHER TAMARIND TITLES

Dizzy's Walk
Mum's Late
Rainbow House
Starlight
Marty Monster
Jessica
Where's Gran?
Toyin Fay
Yohance and the Dinosaurs
Time for Bed
Dave and the Tooth Fairy
Kay's Birthday Numbers
Mum Can Fix It
Ben Makes a Cake
Kim's Magic Tree
Time to Get Up
Finished Being Four
ABC – I Can Be
I Don't Eat Toothpaste Anymore
Giant Hiccups
Boots for a Bridesmaid
Are We There Yet?
Kofi and the Butterflies
Abena and the Rock – Ghanaian Story
The Snowball Rent – Scottish Story
Five Things to Find –Tunisian Story
Just a Pile of Rice – Chinese Story

For older readers, ages 9 – 12
Black Profiles Series
Benjamin Zephaniah
Lord Taylor of Warwick
Dr Samantha Tross
Malorie Blackman
Baroness Patricia Scotland
Mr Jim Braithwaite

A Tamarind Book

Published by Tamarind Ltd, 1999

Edited by Simona Sideri

ISBN 1 870516 39 7

Designed and typeset by Judith Gordon
Printed in Singapore